Thumbelina

Illustrated by Valentina Belloni

Once there was a woman
who didn't have any children.
She really wanted a little girl.

One day, an old woman came to see her.

"Plant this seed," said the old woman. "Soon you will have a little girl."

So the woman planted the seed, and very soon, there was a flower. When the flower opened, out came a little girl. The woman took the little girl into her home.

11

"You are as little as my thumb," said the woman, "so I shall call you Thumbelina."

The woman looked after Thumbelina, and Thumbelina was happy.

One day, a toad saw
Thumbelina playing.

"What a pretty little girl!"
said the toad. "I shall take
her home with me. She will
marry my son."

So the toad took Thumbelina
away. She put Thumbelina
on a lily leaf and went to look
for her son.

But Thumbelina was very
unhappy. She didn't want to
marry a toad! She wanted
to be back at home.

Just then, a butterfly flew by.

"Please help me," said
Thumbelina. "The toad
wants me to marry her son,
but I don't want to. I want
to go home."

The butterfly flew down to the lily leaf. Thumbelina jumped on to the butterfly's back, and they flew to a wood.

23

Thumbelina was very happy in the wood. She lived there all summer. But when winter came, all the butterflies flew away. Thumbelina was all alone.

A mouse came by.

"Please help me," said Thumbelina. "I'm cold and I don't have a home."

The mouse said, "Come and live with me."

The winter was very long
and very cold.

"Soon there won't be any food for
you," said the mouse. "You should
marry the mole. He has food."

29

Thumbelina was very unhappy again. She didn't want to marry the mole and live down a dark tunnel with him!

When the mole came he said, "Come and see my little home in the tunnel. You will be happy there."

So Thumbelina went to see the mole's home.

In the mole's tunnel, Thumbelina saw a swallow who was hurt.

"All of my friends flew away when winter came," said the swallow. "I'm all alone."

Thumbelina looked after
the swallow all winter.
When summer came, the
swallow was better and
he flew away to be with
his friends.

Once again, Thumbelina
was all alone.

"Soon it will be winter. I will
have to marry the mole and live
down in his dark tunnel again,"
she said.

Just then, Thumbelina's swallow flew down to her.

"Come with me," he said. "I will take you to the Land of Summer."

So Thumbelina jumped on to the swallow's back and they flew away.

The Land of Summer was full of flowers. In each of the flowers lived a little boy or girl, just like Thumbelina.

"Thumbelina, you are one of us," they said. "Come and live with us!"

They took Thumbelina
to see their prince.

The prince said, "Will you
marry me, Thumbelina?"

Thumbelina said, "Yes."

So Thumbelina and the prince
lived happily ever after.

How much do you remember about
the story of Thumbelina? Answer these
questions and find out!

- What happens when the
  woman plants the seed?

- Who wants Thumbelina to
  marry her son?

- Can you name one animal that
  Thumbelina lives with?

- Where does the swallow
  take Thumbelina?

- Who does Thumbelina
  marry in the end?

Look at the different story sentences and match them to the people who said them.

"Soon you will have a little girl."

"You are as little as my thumb."

"I shall take her home with me. She will marry my son."

"Come and live with me."

"Please help me."

"Will you marry me, Thumbelina?"

Tick the books you've read!

Level 3

Puss in Boots ☐ | Angry Birds: Matilda Saves the Day ☐ | Sharks ☐ | Thumbelina ☐ | Aladdin ☐ | You won't like this present as much as I DO! ☐ | The Elves and the Shoemaker ☐

Jack and the Beanstalk ☐ | Furi on Music Island ☐ | Poppet Stows Away ☐ | Rapunzel ☐ | The Red Knight ☐ | The Jungle Book ☐ | Roxy and the Great Escape ☐

Hansel and Gretel ☐ | Harry and the Bucketful of Dinosaurs ☐ | Angry Birds: Bomb's Best Birthday ☐ | Angry Birds: Cheer Up, Chuck! ☐

Level 4

Dick Whittington ☐ | Knights and Castles ☐ | Peter and the Wolf ☐ | Pinocchio ☐ | I am Inventing an Invention ☐ | Harry and the Dinosaurs United ☐ | Heidi ☐

Katsuma and the Art Thief ☐ | Luvli and the Glump-a-tron ☐ | The Pied Piper of Hamelin ☐ | Sam and the Robots ☐ | Snow White and the Seven Dwarfs ☐ | The Wizard of Oz ☐ | The Little Mermaid ☐

Alice in Wonderland ☐ | Oddie The Hero ☐ | Angry Birds: Red and the Great Fling Off ☐ | Angry Birds: Stella ☐